Amelia's LONGEST, BIGGEST, MOST-FIGHTS-EVER FAMILY REUNION

by Marissa Moss

(and daughter, sister, half-sister, niece, cousin, stepdaughter, granddaughter Amelia!)

Simon & Schuster Books for Young Readers

New York London Toronto Sydney

That's what my dad was for most of my life — a big fat question mark. All I knew about him was that he left when Cleo, my sister, was two and I was just a baby. Mom must have been really mad at him because she never told us ANYTHING about him. It was like he didn't even exist. Or maybe _we_ didn't exist for him. I mean, if he wanted to find us, he could have figured out a way. But he didn't.

_I_ was the one who finally found _him_. I nagged and super-nagged Mom until she gave me his name and address. I was excited to see he actually lived somewhere besides my imagination, but I was also FURIOUS at Mom. She knew where he was ALL ALONG — she just wouldn't tell me or Cleo.

MOM
I don't know why you want to write to him. He's never written to you.
Maybe he DID write to me, but Mom never gave me his letters. How would I know?
All you've ever gotten from him was your name. He picked out Amelia for Amelia Earhart. Don't expect anything or you'll be disappointed.
I'm just saying...
Just because she hates my dad doesn't mean I have to.

So I wrote him a letter – actually, a comic strip – telling him I was wondering who he was and why he went away. That was hard, but even harder was waiting for him to answer. Part of me was afraid he wouldn't, part of me was afraid he'd tell me to leave him alone, and a teeny, tiny part of me was hoping he'd tell me how much he loved and missed me.

He didn't do any of those things. When I finally got a letter back, he said he was sorry and wanted to be in my life and he invited me to visit him in Chicago, where he lives. But he didn't say he loved me. He just signed the letter "Dad."

What could I do? I went to Chicago. That was last year. I've seen him a couple of times since then and we e-mail and talk on the phone. I know he's trying to be a good dad, and I'm not mad at him anymore, but I still think he should have been there when I was little. He could have tried. So could have Mom. They both say they have their reasons, but I think they're lame excuses.

Dad's version

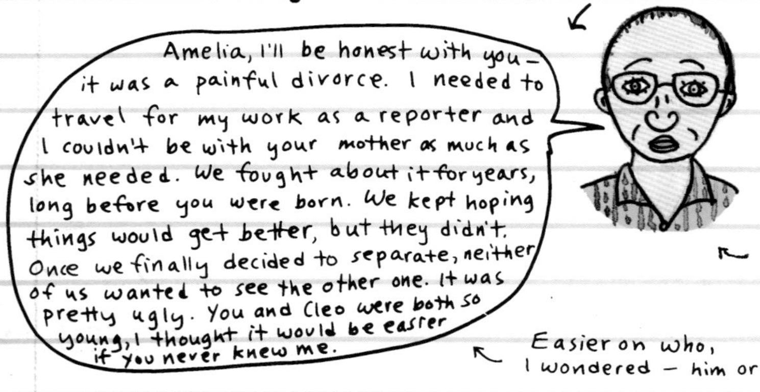

Amelia, I'll be honest with you – it was a painful divorce. I needed to travel for my work as a reporter and I couldn't be with your mother as much as she needed. We fought about it for years, long before you were born. We kept hoping things would get better, but they didn't. Once we finally decided to separate, neither of us wanted to see the other one. It was pretty ugly. You and Cleo were both so young, I thought it would be easier if you never knew me.

When we first met in Chicago, he was really nervous. So was I. I didn't know what to expect, what kind of dad he would be, and what it would feel like to call someone "Dad."

Easier on who, I wondered – him or us?

Even though he'd remarried and had a baby, my half-brother, George, he didn't know how to be a dad to _me_. When he picked me up from the airport, he brought me a teddy bear, like I was a baby or something.

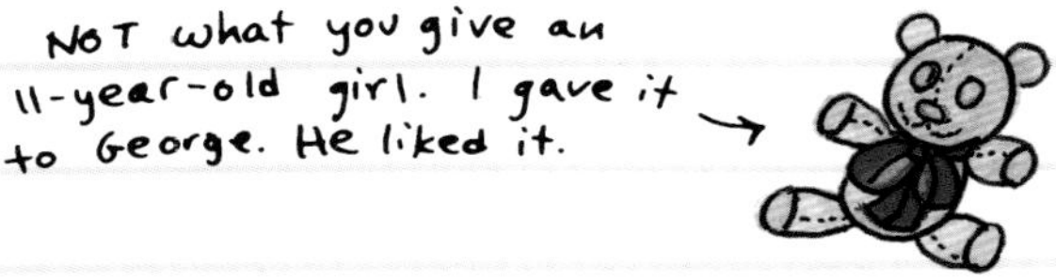

NOT what you give an 11-year-old girl. I gave it to George. He liked it.

He didn't give me what I really wanted — a hug. But we're both better at that stuff now. He tells me he loves me and hugs me. He's better at teasing me and getting my sense of humor. He still has awful taste in clothes when he buys me stuff, but he's learning. And he's told me more about why he left and why he didn't try to see us. Part of it was for our sake, part of it was because Mom was _really_ mad at him.

Mom's version
It was a BIG mistake right from the beginning, but I kept on trying, I really did.
We were seeing a counselor, trying to work things out when you were born. But it all got worse, not better. Quentin wanted out and out he went. I was so ANGRY, I couldn't stand the sound of his voice. I wanted no contact— NONE!

When Mom first told me this, it made me feel terrible, like it was my fault they got divorced. Maybe they could have stayed together if they'd only had one kid to handle. Then I got mad at Mom. Maybe Dad would have helped if she'd let him. I mean, was that fair to Cleo and me?

Anyway, Carly, my best friend, says no one can understand what goes on in a marriage - the good and the bad - except the people in it. Her parents aren't divorced. They have a really good marriage (at least it looks that way to me, on the outside), but her mom is an expert on broken marriages because that's her job, marriage counseling. (She calls it couples therapy, but it's the same thing.) When I told Ms. Tremain about meeting my dad for the first time (that I can remember), she had some great advice.

Amelia, you need to build your own relationship with your dad based on your experiences with him, not on what your mom says.
Even after all these years, your mom still has a lot of anger and resentment. Without realizing it, she may say things to sabotage your relationship with your dad. That kind of thing can happen.

She also said there was no point in blaming either of them for the past. The question was, what kind of future did I want to have with them? I still can't help being angry about it all, but I'm trying to think about what I want <u>now</u>. That's hard-enough work!

Ever since my visit, my dad's been figuring out how to get me back into his life. I'm figuring out <u>if</u> I want to be there.

It's a lot to get used to! There's not just Dad, there's his second wife, Clara, not my favorite person in the world, and their baby, George (who, I admit, is one of my favorite people—he's so adorable!). And there's all the family attached to them—aunts, uncles, cousins, grandparents—all of them to consider.

For most of my life, I had a very small family—just me, Cleo, and Mom. When we went to family gatherings, it was still pretty small.

Cleo

She takes up a LOT of space even if she's just one person. She's LOUD and BOSSY and PUSHY.

Mom

She's mostly quiet, not the chattiest person, but once she starts lecturing—WATCH OUT!

Me

I'm the creative spark of the family. Without me, things would be totally out of balance.

Aunt Lucy—she's the opposite of Mom in every way. Mom's super-organized and controlled. Lucy always forgets basic stuff—like packing a toothbrush or leaving the oven on.

Raisa—she's the little girl Aunt Lucy adopted from Russia when she was 3. Now she's 5 and her English is pretty good but she's shy and doesn't say much.

Uncle Frank—like Lucy, he's never been married, and I think I know why. He's one of the most booooring people I've ever met. But he's family, so I have to listen to his dull, dull stories.

Looking at that family picture, I can't help noticing that Mom AND both her siblings are single. That can't be a coincidence! One thing's for sure – I'm NOTHING like Mom or Lucy or Frank, so maybe there's hope for me.

The last time we all got together was for Thanksgiving. It was fun to play with Raisa, especially since we hardly ever see her, but mostly it was dull and predictable.

The 5 Things That Happen at Every Family Event

① Uncle Frank will argue with Aunt Lucy about whether fluoride is good for your teeth or a government plot to poison us.

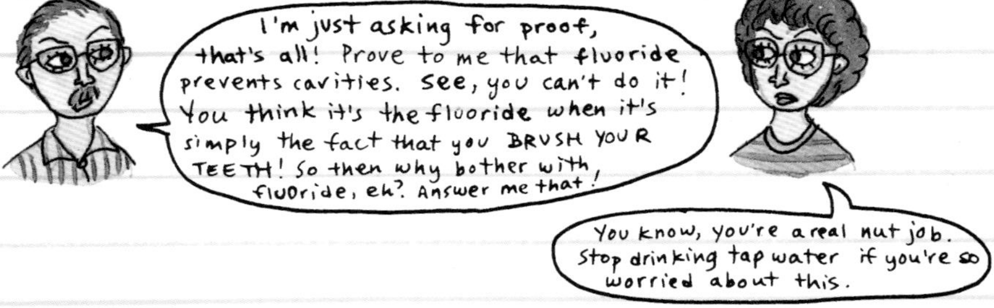

I'm just asking for proof, that's all! Prove to me that fluoride prevents cavities. See, you can't do it! You think it's the fluoride when it's simply the fact that you BRUSH YOUR TEETH! So then why bother with fluoride, eh? Answer me that!
You know, you're a real nut job. Stop drinking tap water if you're so worried about this.

② The main dish – no matter WHAT it is, turkey, meatloaf, brisket, or chicken – will be overcooked and dry.

I don't know what happened this time. I didn't have the oven on too high, I'm sure of that.
Can SOMEONE in this family learn to cook? Every time it's the same thing – a main dish of SAWDUST!

(3) Mom will eat too much dessert and moan about it for the rest of the week.

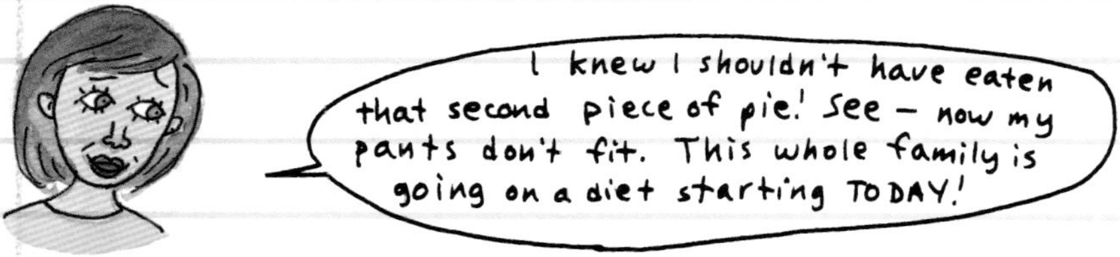

I knew I shouldn't have eaten that second piece of pie! See – now my pants don't fit. This whole family is going on a diet starting TODAY!

(4) There will be leftovers for at least a week that will reappear at every meal in different disguises.

First, it's string beans almondine.
Then it becomes string bean frittata.
Then it's transformed into mushed bean casserole

Mom thinks that putting lots of cheese on something is enough to make it edible, but some things are too far gone for that.

(5) Cleo will say SOMETHING that makes me want to sink into the floor. (Actually this happens WAY more often than at family gatherings – it's just more embarrassing then.)

That reminds me of the time Amelia's bathing suit came off when she tried the high dive. I warned her that bikinis and diving don't mix, but did she listen? Of course not! It was SO FUNNY!!
Yeah, a real laugh riot.

Okay, it can be painfully boring or embarrassing, but at least I'm used to that kind of family gathering. Now suddenly with my dad I'm part of a HUGE family and in a few weeks I'm going to meet <u>all</u> of them — ALL AT ONCE! They're having an enormous family reunion and, according to Dad, that means Cleo and me now too. What will it be like, facing so many strangers at the same time? It sounds worse than the first day at a new school! I mean, it's one thing to find a place for a dad in my life AND a stepmom AND a half-brother. Now I have to fit in all these other people too? UGH!!

Dad ↓

↑ When I first met him, I thought "Yucch! He looks like Cleo with hairy hands!" But he's like me, too, because we both love to write. He's a reporter for the <u>Chicago Tribune</u>, and when he saw my notebook, he said he'd had one just like it when he was a kid.

George ↓

↑ The first time I saw my baby half-brother, he was about 6 months old. Now he's almost 2 years old and he can walk and talk. He calls me "Mia" because "Amelia" is too hard for him to say, which is better than what he calls Cleo — "Eeoh."

Clara ↓

Dad's second wife ↑ (at least I think she's his second one. For all I know he's been married a dozen times). She's a veterinarian, which you would think would make her a super nice person, but you'd be thinking WRONG! She tries way too hard, which just makes her trying.

It's a different family, but I bet there will still be a bunch of predictable things that happen every time they get together. Without knowing anybody, I can guess what some of those things will be. I'm placing bets with Carly on these. If I'm right, she owes me a banana split.

① Somebody will exclaim how great it is that everyone could come. They will use the word "special" at least five times.

And what makes today SO special is that everyone is here!
YOU are the ones who make these special events so...so...SPECIAL!
The special gift of sharing with each other is what makes this a special time. It's all SO special!

② Some kid will get hurt (not badly) and cry ... and cry.

WAAAH!
WAAAAH!
There, there! It's only a scratch. Let's not ruin our special day.

③ Something will be broken. Or spilled. Or both.

④ Somebody's feelings will be hurt.

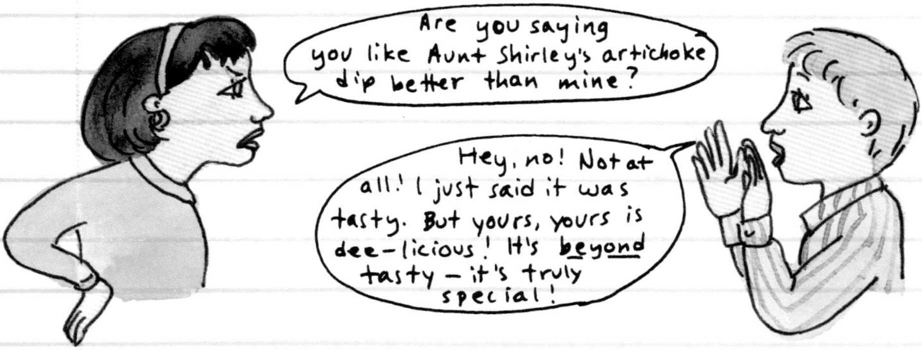

⑤ Something will be forgotten.

Then there's also my grandparents, great-aunts, great-uncles, and cousins once, twice, and thrice removed. It's way too many people to remember. The worst part is they've all known each other their whole lives. Cleo and I don't know ANYBODY! We hardly know our own dad!

I just had a HORRIBLE thought – the only person there I'll feel comfortable with is CLEO!! That can only be an omen of doom!

That's if I go, of course. Mom says we can stay home if we want.

I understand completely if you don't want to go, and I'm sure your father would too.
It's a lot of strange people to have to face all at once. And I do mean strange.

She doesn't sound terribly fond of Dad's family either.

I didn't want to give Mom the satisfaction of convincing me to stay home, but I wasn't sure I wanted to go. Until Cleo gave me no choice.

Of course I'm going! I had a great time last summer when I visited Dad. I can't wait to meet everyone else.
And I really like Clara. She took me to work with her one day and I got to feed some Great Dane puppies. It was so much fun!

Naturally Cleo and Clara hit it off. Why didn't I notice it before? Their names are almost the same! I'll just call them the Clones (or the Clowns) from now on.

If Cleo's going, obviously I have to go too - even though having her around will make a bad situation way WORSE. Watching her butter up Clara will give me major indigestion. Still, that's better than watching her butter up Dad. And that's better than staying home and letting her become the favorite daughter while I become the far-away, don't-care-about-her daughter.

Anyway, she can be Clara's favorite. I don't care about that. I want to be George's favorite.

He's such an adorable toddler now. I love the way he walks, like his diaper is weighing him down and making him off-balance. When I kiss him on his belly button, he has the best laugh - it makes me smile deep inside.

He even knows some words. Here's some basic George vocabulary:

Baa - his favorite stuffed lamb

La la - his word for light or lamp

Ni-ni - his word for night-night or go to sleep

When I see my dad with George, I think he's a great father. But it makes me sad, too, because he wasn't that kind of father for <u>me</u>. On the plus side, Clara's not that kind of mother for me either. She's just a stepmother (which really means nothing except that she's married to my dad). Mom has her problems, but compared to Clara, she's Mary Poppins.

← There are certain things a step-mother should never do. Here's a quick list. →

roll-your-eyes face reserved for Moms only →

MOTHER

(Yes, a mother can do these things even if you hate it. Come on, she's your <u>mother</u>.)

1. Nag you to clean up your room — you don't have to listen, but she has the right to bug you about it.

2. Make embarrassing suggestions about how to clear up your acne, improve your posture, or select a deodorant.

3. Hug and kiss you in public. I know — it's gross. Just remember, other kids' mothers do it to them!

STEPMOTHER

(No, a stepmother can NEVER do this unless you say it's okay. It's YOUR choice, not hers.)

1. Nag you about your grades, studying, tests, homework, ANYTHING to do with school.

2. Tell you about the facts of life — PLEASE! That's what sex ed. in school is for. It's bad enough coming from a parent, but a stepparent — NEVER!

3. Criticize your hair, clothes, taste in music, anything <u>personal</u> that's none of her business.

So it's all set. Cleo and I will have our first plane trip together with no grown-up around. I hope it's better than sitting next to Cleo on the bus for a field trip — at least then I can open a window to escape her carsick fumes. She'd better <u>not</u> get airsick! If she does, I'm spending the whole flight standing in the back of the plane by the toilets (usually not the best-smelling part of an airplane, but compared to puking Cleo, it'll be a breath of fresh air).

I wrote to Nadia about it. She's the one who encouraged me to find my dad in the first place, so in a way she's responsible for all of this happening — meeting Dad, finding a whole new family, the family reunion, all of it.

Dear Nadia,
Guess what? Cleo and I are going to a big family reunion in Dallas. It's not for Mom's family. It's for Dad's. So I'll meet all these uncles, aunts, and cousins for the first time. And my grandparents! It's strange to think I suddenly have all these people in my life. Except I'm not sure yet if I really do. Just because you're related to someone doesn't mean you have to care about them. So will they care about me? *Yours till the criss crosses,* *amelia*

Nadia Kurz
61 South St.
Barton, CA
91010

Cleo is totally excited. I'm not so sure. Yeah, I like to see new places and stay in hotels, but not with Cleo. Who can sleep with her snoring? And I'm not crazy about meeting a bunch of strangers. Like I wrote to Nadia, just because they're family doesn't mean I'll like them — or that they'll like me!

This is going to be SO COOL! We'll stay in a hotel and swim in the pool and meet all our family. I'm sure they can't wait to get to know me!

← Sometimes I wish I was like Cleo. She never worries about anything. And NOTHING embarrasses her.

But I'm not Cleo so I can't help feeling nervous. Carly, my best friend, tried to convince me it would be great. I wish she could come with me — then it would be great. Even if no one else talked to me, I'd have her. Now all I have is Cleo, which is like saying all I have is zero or a negative number.

Amelia, you're going to love it. It's always fun to explore a new city, and you've never been to Dallas. And you'll meet some interesting people, I bet.

Carly thinks my dad is great just because he's a reporter and that's what she wants to be when she grows up. So naturally she thinks the rest of his family is also wonderful. I hope she's right — or at least not too wrong.

What if Carly's wrong? What if they're not interesting people? What if they're the most BOOOOOOORING people on the planet? Or what if they fight and yell a lot? Or are plain annoying like Cleo, talking with their mouths full and singing off-key? What if I'm trapped in a room full of Cleos?! What a nightmare!

Cleos of all ages, boys and girls, in a horrible sing-along
KUMBAYA KUMBAYA!
Grandma Cleos, Grandpa Cleos, baby Cleos, Uncle Cleos, Aunt Cleos, cousin Cleos
HELP!

I'll never survive.

I had to get that image OUT of my head. So I made flash cards of all the possible types of relatives that are NOT Cleo clones. That way I can be on the alert and know who to avoid (and not think of facing a massive crowd of Cleos).

The Cheek Pincher

The Head Patter or Hair Rumpler

The Long-Boring-Pointless-Story Teller

The Too-Many-Nosy-Questions Prying Busy-Body

The Stern, Rigid, Don't-Touch-That Police
Be careful you don't break anything! NO! Don't go near that! Keep your hands to yourself!
The Shove-Food-Into-You-Constantly Feeder
Just try a bite. It's deee-licious! Here, have some. Come on! One bite, just one!
It's so nice to see you, such a special treat!
It's very special that you came. It makes this
a REAL reunion. Really!
Help! You're sucking in all my air!
The Suspicious All-Kids-Are-Trouble Grump
I know your kind! Swilling soda all the time, eyes glued to the TV, listening to your "music!"
You need some exercise, little missy, some good, hard work!
The Gushy, Too-Close-to-you Talker
The Too-Much-Perfume Hugger
GASP!
Now, give us a hug!
I need a gas mask!

I showed Carly my deck of familycards. She laughed but then she said I wasn't being fair – where were all the good types of people? I told her I don't have to worry about them. Still, she had a point, so I added a few more cards.

I made up the cousin and aunt stuff because I don't know yet if I have relatives like that. But Carly does, so I know they exist. At least I know George, the cute baby, will be there, so SOMEBODY will be nice to me. And with so many cousins, at least one should be okay.

Finally I added Dad, Clara, Cleo, and me.

The Clueless Dad Who Wants Some Kind of Relationship with You But Isn't Sure What or How Yet
I'm trying, Amelia.
Give me some time.

The Annoying Stepmom Who Tries WAY TOO HARD to Be an Instant Best Friend
I know just how you feel!
Want to go shopping with me at the mall?

The Obnoxious Sister Who's an Expert at Saying the Wrong Thing at the Wrong Time
Wow, that was some fart, Amelia!

The I'm-Not-Sure-About-All-This-Please-Don't-Force-Anything-On-Me Sister (me)
where do I belong in this family?

After all that worrying, it turned out I didn't worry ENOUGH. Mom took us to the airport and we got on the plane and I was just beginning to think that MAYBE this would be a fun trip after all when Cleo took a bunch of papers out of her purse and started reading them. I wouldn't have paid much attention, but she was grinning and laughing — way too happy for ordinary reading. I had to ask her what was so funny.

"Just some e-mails I printed out," she said.

"Why bother to do that? Who are they from?" I asked.

"One of our cousins, Justin. We've been e-mailing and messaging ever since my last visit to see Dad. Didn't you meet him when you went? He's SO sweet!"

My stomach sank. No, I hadn't met him. I had no idea who he was. And now he and Cleo were good buddies and I would be the ONLY person who didn't know anybody. I didn't say anything. I didn't want to admit that Dad had done stuff with Cleo he hadn't done with me (like seeing cousins and aunts and uncles). But I couldn't lie, either, or Cleo would find out.

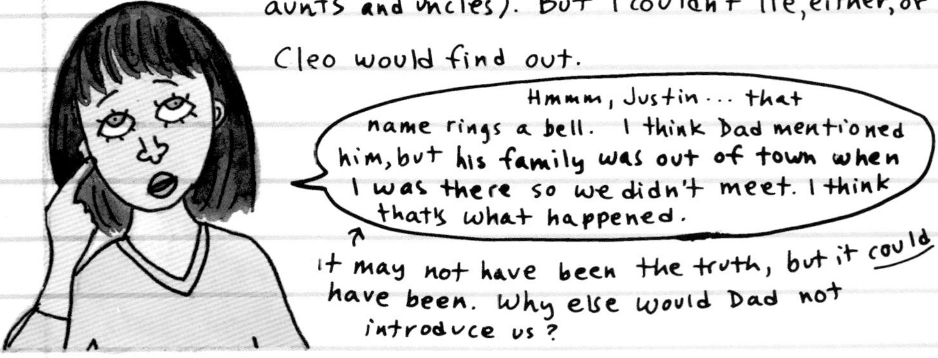
Hmmm, Justin... that name rings a bell. I think Dad mentioned him, but his family was out of town when I was there so we didn't meet. I think that's what happened.
It may not have been the truth, but it could have been. Why else would Dad not introduce us?

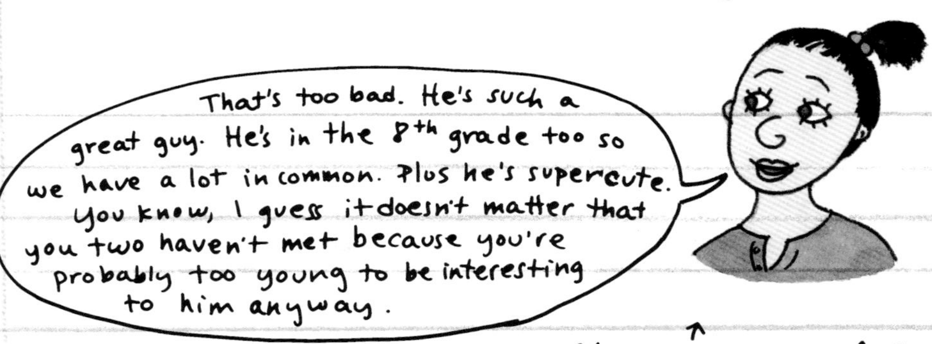

That's too bad. He's such a great guy. He's in the 8th grade too so we have a lot in common. Plus he's supercute. You know, I guess it doesn't matter that you two haven't met because you're probably too young to be interesting to him anyway.

Cleo has a knack for the cutting remark - OUCH!

I rolled my eyes. Thanks a LOT, Cleo, I thought. Like you're automatically friends with someone just because they're the same age as you. We all know how true that is! As if the whole 8th-grade class are your friends! And as if I'm automatically boring just because I'm in 6th grade. I'm waaaaay more interesting than Cleo, no matter what! I just have to prove that to Justin - and to everyone else.

I hunkered down in my seat and stared out the window. I tried NOT to pay attention to Cleo's snorts and giggles. No way was I going to ask her what was so funny.

This was going to be the longest weekend ever - and not in a good way. I tried to shut Cleo out. I tried <u>not</u> to think about cousins and uncles and aunts. It was enough worrying about a dad, a stepmom, and a part-time brother.

I couldn't help remembering the first time I saw Dad. There was a strange man waiting for me at the airport in Chicago and I knew from his jelly-roll nose that he had to be my dad. I had tried to imagine his face and voice so many times and there he was, right in front of me. He wasn't ANYTHING like I'd imagined. I wanted to run back onto the plane and go home. I wanted to walk right past him and pick out some other, better guy to be my dad. But I didn't. I just stood there until he came over and said, "Hi, you must be Amelia."

It was SO awkward.

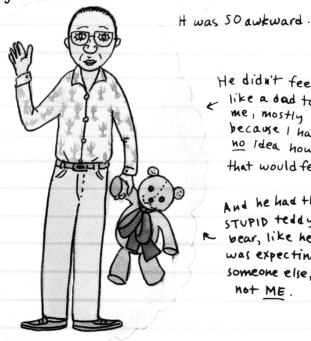

when I first saw him, neither of us knew what to say, we were both so nervous.

He didn't feel like a dad to me, mostly because I had no idea how that would feel.

I couldn't help noticing how hairy his hands were, but I was polite and shook his hand anyway.

And he had that STUPID teddy bear, like he was expecting someone else, not ME.

I'm still not completely comfortable with Dad, but it's a lot easier to be with him now. We're getting used to each other. And now I know that with me first times are usually awkward and tense, not fun and exciting. I just have to remind myself that there's only <u>one</u> first time at a particular thing — after that I've done it before. So no matter how icky this reunion thing is, I might as well get it over with — and the <u>next</u> time I see these people, it'll be <u>much</u> better.

The flight was pretty short and I didn't have to listen to Cleo guffawing for too long when the plane started to land. As soon as we got off the plane, we saw people with cowboy boots and hats. I guess that's how you know you're in Dallas.

Dad was waiting for us, along with Clara and George. At least this time there was no teddy bear.

Cleo!
Amelia!

CLEO! You're so beautiful and grown up now! Amelia, nice to see you.

Dad had a big smile on his face — he sure wasn't nervous <u>this</u> time. First he hugged Cleo. Then he hugged me. Do I always have to come second in EVERYTHING? At least he was happy to see me — that part was good.

EE-O! MIA!

Clara was gushing all over Cleo — it was enough to make me queasy. How come she says Cleo's beautiful and not me?

Even George was happy to see Cleo. I bet if I'd stayed home, no one would have missed me.

Cleo, of course, was beaming.

Dad! Clara! Georgie!

She was supernice and polite, like a totally different person. Now I get it — they think they know and like Cleo, but that's not the real Cleo. It's a pod person, a fake.

The whole way to the hotel, Cleo chattered on and on. I just talked to George. No one talked to me.

Until Dad asked me how I liked Dallas. I said I didn't know yet, all I'd seen was highways and billboards (and the cowboy hats and boots in the airport).

"Well, tomorrow we'll see a real slice of Texas. The family reunion is at an old ranch just outside of town. There'll be hay rides and square dancing and, of course, all the barbeque you can eat."

Yeehaw, I thought. But I didn't say it. If Cleo could be polite, so could I.

"Cool!" Cleo said. "Can I get cowboy boots and a cowboy hat? I want to look like a real Texan!"

I snorted. The only thing she would look like was a real jerk.

But Clara thought it was a great idea. "We should all do that," she said. "Don't you agree, Quentin?"

Dad nodded. "That's the spirit. This is going to be the biggest, best family reunion ever — because you girls are here!"

Cleo smiled. I meant to smile. I tried to smile, but it came out all lopsided. Some things you just can't fake.

Usually I love hotels, but by the time we got to our room I was in a really bad mood. And it just got worse. We weren't staying in a regular room. It was a suite, so Dad and Clara had the bedroom with a crib put in there for George, and Cleo and I were supposed to sleep in the other room on the sofa bed.

IN THE SAME BED!!!!....

There aren't enough exclamation marks in the world to convey how awful that thought was.

I said I could sleep on the floor. I said I could sleep in the bathtub. I said I could even sleep in the lobby — ANYWHERE, so long as I didn't have to share a bed with Cleo.

Clara glared at me. "You're both girls. What's the big deal here? I often shared a bed with my sister when we traveled."

That's you, I thought, not me. And that's your sister, NOT Cleo.

Here's the problem:

HAZARDS OF CLEO

But I couldn't say all that without sounding like a brat. Meanwhile Cleo wore her most angelic face.

It's fine with me to share a bed with Amelia.
I don't mind at all. She can even choose which side she wants.

As if *she*'s the reasonable, nice daughter and I'm NOT!

If I'd known that I'd have to share a bed with Cleo, I DEFINITELY would NOT have come, even if that meant she got to be Dad's favorite. Some things are just not worth it.

But I was already here, so I gritted my teeth and rolled up an extra blanket to go down the center of the fold-out sofa bed. It wasn't the brick wall I wanted, but it was better than nothing.

"Good!" Dad clapped his hands. "I'm glad that's settled. Now we can get our cowboy duds and have some Tex-Mex food for dinner." He used the fake, too-cheery voice he had when we first met. I guess that meant he wasn't comfortable with what was happening.

Good, I thought, glaring at him. I shouldn't be the only one who's miserable. I hope Cleo's snoring is so loud, it keeps him and Clara up all night. That'll show them!

On the way to the car, Cleo and Clara walked together, whispering back and forth. How did they get to be so buddy-buddy? I suppose I should have been glad because that meant Dad had to walk with me, but I got the feeling he was stuck with me more than wanting to be with me.

It's strange, but with Mom, in the Mom-Amelia-Cleo family, I'm the good daughter, the easier one, and Cleo's the one who exasperates Mom and gets on her nerves. In _this_ family, the Dad–Clara-George–Cleo-Amelia one, _I'm_ the problem child. How did _that_ happen?

Who's going to be a big, handsome cowboy? Who is?
Is it Georgie Boy? Is George going to be a cowboy? Yes, he is! He is!

I didn't even try to talk to Dad. My mood was going from bad to worse, from black to blacker.

Dad didn't talk to me either. He just talked to George, another "good" child.

When I was little, I had a mood ring that changed colors according to what I was feeling. At least that's what it was supposed to do. Usually it was dark gray or black, even when I was happy. Now I think it was because I have cold hands, but then I thought the colors really meant something. Anyway, moods are much more complicated than the five choices on the mood ring (sad, happy, jealous, angry, in love). If I invented a ring like that, I'd have a way more complicated scale with LOTS more colors.

Basic Moods

Happy · Sad · Mad · Bored · Scared

Subtle Moods

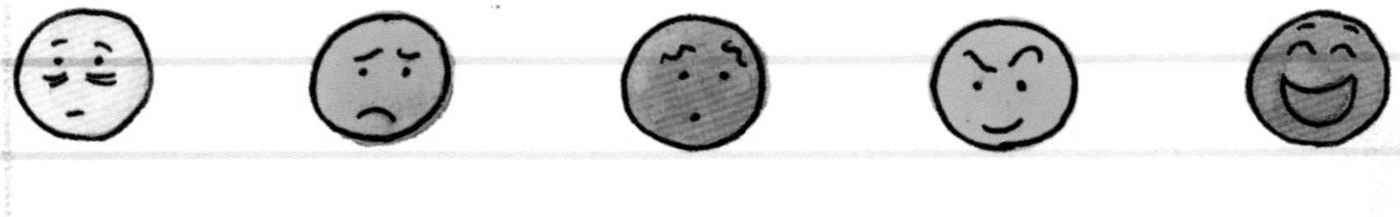

Tired · Skeptical · Confused · Sneaky · Thrilled

MOOD MEASURE

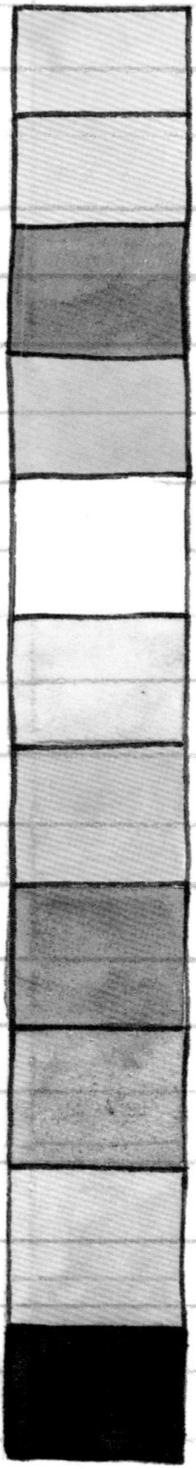

← On top of the world! Everything's perfect and you're superhappy, like you just won the lottery.

← You're feeling really good, like nothing can go wrong and the future is one long summer vacation.

← You're happy, like you just finished a great book (or, better yet, <u>started</u> one) or ate an ice cream cone.

← You haven't had dessert yet but you know it's coming.

← You just woke up and the day could go either way. Right now it's not good, but it's not bad, either.

← You're a little annoyed, like you stubbed your toe. It's not a big deal — yet!

← You're mad enough to yell and snap but not so mad as to throw things.

← You're furious, out-of-contral angry — steam is coming out of your ears.

← You're sad and feel all wilty, like old, limp lettuce.

← You're frustrated, like when no matter how many times you explain something, your mom just doesn't get it.

← You're sad and mad and frustrated all together. You feel like no one loves you and no one ever will. It's the worst feeling EVER!

I would rate Dad's mood a white, George's a purple, Clara's a pink, and Cleo's a yellow. And I'm a definite deep, deep black—all before we've been here 24 hours. That's got to be a record for mood busting.

We drove into an enormous parking lot dominated by a huge neon cowboy hat. On the roof of the building next to it was a life-size plastic cow.

Roy's Cowboy Emporium
Everything a Dude Needs!

Normally this kind of place would put me in a great mood because it seems like an enormous joke. I mean, a real cowboy store? What would they sell besides hats and boots? Lassos? Chaps and spurs? Saddles? Are there real cowboys anymore? Who buys this stuff—tourists like us, or do people here take cowboys more seriously? I mean, you have to wonder.

Lassos, chaps, spurs, kerchiefs, boots, saddles, belts, bolo ties, hats, suede jackets and vests with fringe at the bottom — you name it, Roy's had it. They even had chewing tobacco and cowboy gum. With all that, I thought I might see a real cowboy in the store shopping for that special something he just had to own. But all I saw were regular people like us who wanted to pretend to be cowboys for a while.

I never knew there were so many kinds of cowboy hats.

brown ones with leather strings

black ones with silver on the band

white ones for the good guys

pink ones with bows

I picked a black one and a blue kerchief.

I thought I looked good. The funny thing is, it's hard to feel bad with a cowboy hat on. For some reason just wearing it made me feel better.

I looked like I was ready for an adventure— a cattle stampede, a thievin' coyote, or a family reunion!

↑ Cleo the cowgirl—or is it just Cleo the cow?

Cleo didn't settle for just the hat and a kerchief. She went whole hog, making Dad buy her a plaid shirt, suede vest, and bright red boots that clashed with her pink hat. I thought she looked ridiculous, but Clara said she was gorgeous, a real Annie Oakley (whoever that is).

I almost felt sorry for Dad, having to spend so much money, but he could have said no. I think he feels guilty he went so many years without giving us even a birthday present, so now he's trying to make up for it. That's fine with me. I figure I'll wait until I'm 16 and ask for a car. That's way better than a bunch of goofy cowboy gear.

They even had a hat and boots small enough for George. He looked SO CUTE! →

George is another reason it's hard to stay in a bad mood. When he smiles at you, it's impossible not to smile back. →

Unfortunately that happy mood didn't last long. It would have been nice to just eat dinner and not talk, but Cleo insisted on asking a zillion questions.

I noticed that her table manners hadn't improved, even if the rest of her behavior was fake nicey-nice. I guess it's too hard for her to fake good eating habits.

I have to admit some of her questions were good ones, things I wanted to know too. But mostly I didn't want to think about all the strangers who I was going to meet tomorrow. I didn't want to know whether they liked me or Mom. I could guess the answer about Mom's opinions. I'm pretty sure she hates Dad and everyone he's related to — including Clara and George.

Dad avoided the questions about Mom, but he answered most of the other ones. I wonder what he thinks about Mom. (I sure know her opinion of him!) He never says anything bad about her, but that doesn't mean he doesn't think those kinds of things.

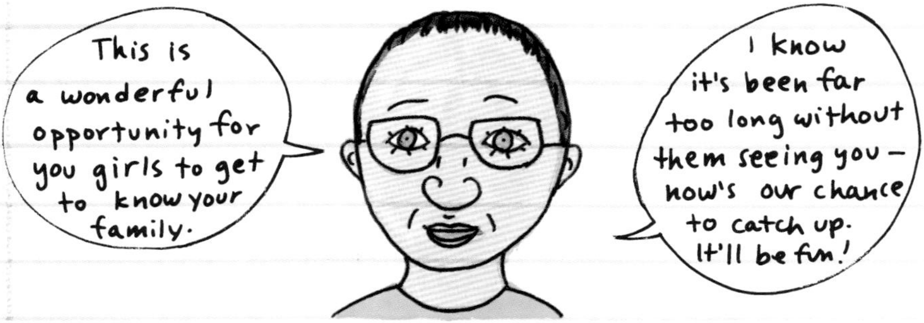

This is a wonderful opportunity for you girls to get to know your family.
I know it's been far too long without them seeing you - now's our chance to catch up. It'll be fun!

Dad likes to focus on the positive.

Clara nodded and chimed in, "It's a lot of people to meet at once. That may make you nervous, but everyone is very nice. I know exactly how you feel because that's what happened to me, too - I met practically the whole family at the same time!"

I glared at her. She had NO idea how I felt - NONE. The last time I visited she invaded my privacy and READ MY NOTEBOOK!! That's a capital offense as far as I'm concerned and proves my point - if she had any sensitivity at all, she would know better. But she didn't. She doesn't. She's absolutely, totally clueless about my feelings.

But Cleo acted like they were soul sisters. I wanted to gag!

You're so right, Clara. Thanks for understanding!
Poor Amelia won't know anyone.
At least I've already met Justin and his family, so they won't all be new faces.

That was it! I snapped!

"Poor Amelia" is just fine! I don't need to know anyone! I don't want to know anyone! I don't know why I bothered to come!

Clara gave me one of her phony, sugary, oh-I'm-so-concerned-about-you smiles. "What can we do to make this easier for you, Amelia? I understand how hard it must be."

"You don't understand anything! "None of you do! Just leave me alone!"" I threw down my napkin and ran to the bathroom.

Luckily it was a fancy bathroom with a sofa in it, the kind that's called a powder room, not a bathroom.

I sat on the sofa and started to cry. The reunion hadn't even begun yet and already everything was going wrong. I wished I hadn't come. I wished I could talk to Carly or Nadia. I wished I had a completely different family, one where there was no divorce.

I stayed there a long time. My eyes were sore from crying and my nose was running. Suddenly I was very tired. All I wanted to do was go to sleep and wake up in my familiar bed in my room at home. Instead I was stuck in a restaurant bathroom in Dallas. What was I going to do?

Someone knocked at the door. I heard Dad's voice. "Amelia, come out. We need to talk."

I didn't want to spend the rest of my life on that sofa, so I got up and opened the door. My knees were stiff and creaky, my cheeks tight with dried tears.

I couldn't look up at Dad or I would start crying again, so I just stood there, staring at his shoes. Now what would happen, I wondered. Would he be mad at me?

Would he send me back to Mom so I wouldn't ruin his big family event? Would he decide that one daughter was enough, he didn't need two? Would he tell me he'd made a terrible mistake answering my letter and he wanted to go back to the way things were before — a great, big silence?

He didn't do or say any of those things. He just hugged me.

It was exactly the right thing to do.

We stood that way for a long time. Neither of us said anything — we didn't need to talk after all. The hug said it better.

Finally Dad pulled himself away and took my hand. "Come on," he said. "It's late. You need to sleep. Tomorrow's a big day."

I nodded. He was right. Tomorrow would be a very big day. I promised myself I'd try to make it a good one. I was here, after all, so I might as well.

That night was the worst night ever. Not because of what happened in the restaurant. Not because of what was going to happen the next day. Because of one big, fat reason—Cleo!

The sofa bed sagged in the middle, rolling Cleo and me together. No matter how much I tried to sleep on the edge of the bed, I couldn't.

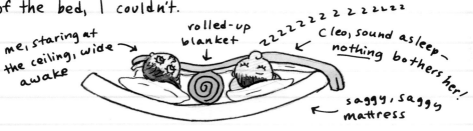

If it weren't for the blanket I'd put between us, we would have been practically on top of each other. As it was, Cleo was way too close to me. I stuck wads of cotton in my ears and I could still hear her snoring. I kept on kicking and pushing at her until finally she rolled over and the snoring stopped. But I couldn't fall asleep. I felt like I was sliding down a cliff—the bed was so caved-in and lumpy. Sleeping on the floor would have been MUCH more comfortable.

I don't remember falling asleep but I must have, because the next thing I knew I had bolted wide-awake, sweating, from a HORRIBLE nightmare.

I dreamed I was in a big corral crowded with people. Everyone was wearing cowboy outfits except me. I was still in my pajamas. I wanted to go home so I could get dressed, but I couldn't find the gate. All I could see were the backs of people with their hats. Everyone was looking at something in the center of the corral.

I squeezed through so I could see what was so interesting. Right in the middle of all those staring, smiling faces was Cleo! She was sitting on a tall stool, playing a guitar and singing.

Even though her singing was screechy and off-key, everyone stamped their feet and clapped their hands. They loved her!

I had to get out of there, but a big man who looked like Dad but wasn't Dad – somehow in the dream I knew he was my uncle – grabbed me and shoved me to the front.

"Now, you behave!" he shouted. "Why can't you be more like your sister?"

"I don't want to be like her!" I yelled.

Suddenly everyone turned to look at me, their eyes red with anger and hatred.

"Get her!" someone shouted.

"Don't let her escape!" someone else screamed.

Hands reached for me from all sides. I panicked. I couldn't get away! I tried to yell for help!

And then I woke up.

What a terrible dream! I was afraid to go back to sleep, so I got up and read my book in the bathroom. I seemed to be spending a lot of time in the bathroom these days and I didn't even have diarrhea.

This bathroom didn't have a sofa in it, just a cold tile floor with a small rug on it. This weekend was NOT a relaxing vacation, NOT a fun family visit. It was turning into the longest nightmare ever.

At breakfast Cleo said she'd slept great. Everyone had. Except me.

I could barely keep my eyes open.

I looked like I'd slept under a bed, not on one.

I decided to skip eating and went back to sleep for a couple of hours until Dad woke me up and said it was time to head for the ranch. I had such a bad case of bed head, I was grateful for the cowboy hat - no way I was EVER going to take it off.

I tried not to think about my bad dream and the possibility of it coming true. After all, Cleo doesn't know how to play the guitar. The whole thing was crazy! (Well, she doesn't know how to sing, but she still does.)

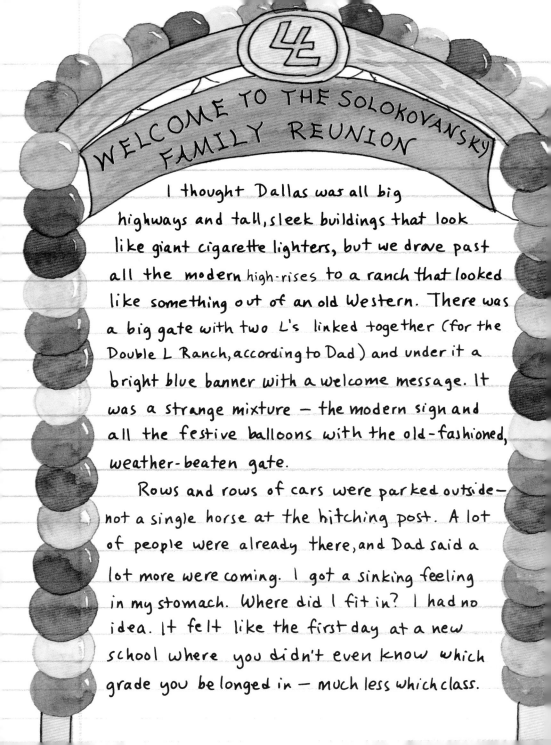

LL
WELCOME TO THE SOLOKOVANSKY
FAMILY REUNION

I thought Dallas was all big highways and tall, sleek buildings that look like giant cigarette lighters, but we drove past all the modern high-rises to a ranch that looked like something out of an old Western. There was a big gate with two L's linked together (for the Double L Ranch, according to Dad) and under it a bright blue banner with a welcome message. It was a strange mixture – the modern sign and all the festive balloons with the old-fashioned, weather-beaten gate.

Rows and rows of cars were parked outside – not a single horse at the hitching post. A lot of people were already there, and Dad said a lot more were coming. I got a sinking feeling in my stomach. Where did I fit in? I had no idea. It felt like the first day at a new school where you didn't even know which grade you belonged in – much less which class.

I put George in his stroller and felt safer being behind it, like he was a kind of shield. I have to admit, I was impressed by Cleo. She seemed totally fearless. Meeting so many strangers didn't faze her at all.

I can't wait for everyone to see how great I look.
I bet no one else has a pink cowboy hat and red boots. This is a real fashion statement.

Either she was incredibly brave or too full of herself to be worried. I wasn't sure which, but either way, I envied her. I wished I could be as calm as her — or like George, completely oblivious to what anyone thinks about him.

I adjusted my hat and tried to look like someone cool and interesting.
But what if there was no one cool and interesting for me to meet?

The first people we ran into were Dad's parents — my grandparents. How ~~weird~~ ~~wierd~~ ~~weird~~ ~~wierd~~ weird!

It was even stranger than the spelling of this annoying word!

For most of my life I didn't have any grandparents. Now here they were.

There you two are! We've been waiting for this moment for so long!
Such grown-up young ladies now!
The last time we saw Amelia, she was little enough to fit inside a shoe box!

My grandmother had Cleo's nose! So that's where it came from! She had bluish hair and bright orange lipstick that made me think of a troll doll. But she wasn't a troll— there was something about her face that was warm and kind.

My grandfather had even less hair on the top of his head than Dad did, but he had these strange long wiry hairs growing out of his eyebrows and ears. He was really old and wrinkled, but his eyes were bright blue and sparkly and young.

I liked them both right away. Maybe deep down my baby self remembered them — we had met before!

Whatever it was, I felt comfortable with them right away. I didn't even mind hugging them. I wanted to call them "Grandma" and "Grandpa," but somehow that was too much. The words stuck in my throat, so I didn't say anything. But I smiled. Maybe this reunion wouldn't be so bad after all.

I wanted to ask a million questions, like did they get along with Mom? Did they try to see us or did they give up like Dad had? Did they visit us a lot before the divorce? Did they approve of Dad marrying Mom in the first place? But I didn't get a chance to ask anything because a big man with a booming voice pushed in front of me to scoop up my grandmother in a bear hug.

I knew he had to be Dad's brother – he had the trademark jelly-roll nose. He looked like the uncle in my nightmare.

I could tell Dad's feelings were hurt — after all, his parents WERE seeing how their grandkids had grown, just different ones than the bellowing man meant.

"Hello, Harold," Dad said. "I'd like to introduce you to my daughters."

Harold turned to us as if just noticing that we existed. He looked at us like he was examining a dent in his brand-new car.

"Chloe? Adelia?" His eyebrows pitched up like they were trying to escape his forehead. "Wow! I forgot you had daughters! What happened? Did that witch of an ex-wife finally let them out of her clutches? Halleluyah, miracles CAN happen!"

I was FURIOUS, but I didn't have to say anything because Dad was even madder than me.

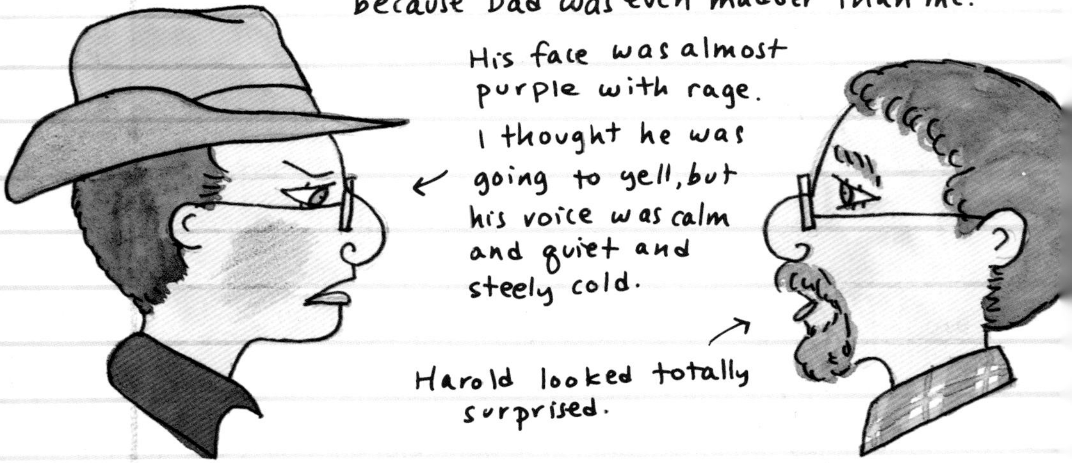

His face was almost purple with rage. I thought he was going to yell, but his voice was calm and quiet and steely cold.
Harold looked totally surprised.

"Harold," Dad hissed through gritted teeth. "I told you the girls were coming. REMEMBER? This is their chance to meet all the family." He put one hand on Cleo's shoulder. "This is Cleo." He said her name **superslowly** and clearly like he was explaining a difficult foreign word. Then he put his other hand on my shoulder. "And this is A<u>m</u>elia. NOT Adelia. And you'll forgive me if I insist that you DON'T insult their mother."

"Oh, hey, sorry," Harold sputtered. "Guess I put my foot in my mouth with that one."

"There's no boot big enough to fill that hole!" Cleo sniped. I was impressed. Go, Cleo, I thought, you tell that jerk! But Dad gripped her shoulder tighter to calm her down.

"Now, now," Harold soothed. "No need to get nasty. We're all family here, aren't we? I said I was sorry, so let's shake and be friends."

Dad nodded. So we did. First Cleo, then me. Yucch! I wanted to wash my hand right away. Then Dad suggested our grandparents take us to get a drink while he and his brother chatted. We didn't need to be asked twice—we were all eager to escape.

I could tell that Cleo was still steamed. It would take a lot of ice to cool her down.

"You have to excuse Harold," Grandma said. (There- I called her Grandma, even if it's only in this notebook.) "He means well. He just doesn't always say the right thing."

"I'll say!" Cleo snapped. "He's a colossal jerk!"

"Come on," Grandpa urged. "He's also your uncle, so you need to see his good side. That's what families do — accept each other, the good and the bad."

Cleo didn't say anything, but she looked at me and I could tell exactly what she was thinking — if this is what it means to have family around then no, thank you! I smiled at her because for once I felt exactly the same as she did.

We found the drinks, passing knots of people on the way who ran up and greeted Grandma and Grandpa or just waved and shouted hello. There were no more introductions and after Cleo and I were settled in a corner sipping sodas, they left us, saying they needed to find our aunts and uncles.

← I put some apple juice in George's sippy cup. The whole drama had passed right by him. Little kids are so lucky!

"This sucks!" Cleo said. "Now they're afraid to talk to us or introduce us to anyone."

"Well, you weren't exactly polite," I pointed out.

"Neither was Harold – and he's a grown-up. He should know better." She slumped back in her chair. "I guess I was expecting everyone to be excited to see us after so long, like we would be the stars of the show. I thought the banner at the gate would say 'Welcome, Cleo and Amelia!' But no one cares that we bothered to come. Harold didn't even remember Dad talking about us!"

Wow. I hadn't imagined anything like that! While I was dreading how horrible this trip would be, Cleo was dreaming of some fantasy, lovey-dovey family reunion. I couldn't help it – I felt bad for her.

She had some kind of Miss America fantasy – like she would be on this big float, blowing kisses at her adoring fans.
Cleo
Miss

The reality had to be a big disappointment. I actually felt sorry for her. That only lasted a minute, though, because some boy came up to us, and Cleo leaped to her feet, grinning, the prom queen once more.

Hey, Justin!
How's it going?
Good. I've been looking all over for you. Wanna see the pond out back? It's kinda cool.
Sure, let's go!

Cleo turned to me. "Tell Dad I'm with Justin."

Justin looked at me like he'd just noticed my existence.

"Oh, is this your sister?" he asked.

"Yeah, that's Amelia." Cleo was already walking away.

And she'd complained about our grandparents not introducing us to anyone! _She_ was way worse! She could have invited me to join them, but instead they were gone, leaving me alone with George. I should have just said I was coming too, I wanted to see the pond. Now I was abandoned.

I looked at George. "Can this get any worse?" I asked. He didn't have an answer. Neither did I.

I got tired of sitting on the itchy hay bale and decided to take George exploring.

What else was there to do? I didn't see Dad anywhere. My grandparents were surrounded by loving children and grandchildren. I didn't belong anywhere.

At least George was having a great time. We found the barn with the cows and a pen with sheep and goats. That was enough to thrill him. He was especially excited about the goats. I wished I was as little as him, back to the age when a smelly goat was my idea of fun, and I didn't care if people paid attention to me as long as I was fed and warm.

There were groups of kids running around, playing with each other, but I didn't know anyone and they all looked younger than me. I couldn't just barge in and join them.

I was tempted to go back to the car and wait for the whole thing to be over. I wished I'd brought my notebook with me, but I'd left it at the hotel. Writing and drawing usually made me feel better. Now all I had to distract me was George and he'd fallen asleep. He was still cute, but not much fun that way.

I bumped the stroller over to the far back pastures and watched the horses. There were a couple of young colts, all knobby knees and gangly legs. I couldn't help it—watching them made me smile.

There was one especially small one who was so young, he had trouble organizing his legs.
He kept on wobbling and falling, then unfolding his legs and trying again.
Finally he got it right. He just stood there, looking really tired.

Then a big lump in the grass next to him moved. It was his mother, standing up. I was surprised because you never see horses lying down – they sleep standing up. Then I realized why the colt was having so much trouble with his legs – he must have just been born! That's why the mare had been lying down.

I climbed over the fence and walked slowly over to them. The mare looked at me and snorted, but she let me come close. I could see the foal was still wet from being inside of her. His hooves were soft and spongy and new, not yet hard. I held my breath, touching the colt gently. I felt like I'd been given a gift from the universe, to see someone so soon after they'd entered the world.

Then the mare ambled off and her baby followed. I stood there watching them, full of a strange, calm wonder. It was magical.

"You know how to ride?" The voice startled me. It came from a girl who was sitting on the fence next to George's stroller.

I walked up, shaking my head. "Not horses," I said. "Bikes, yes. I'm not from around here."

"Me neither," the girl said. "We live in Chicago. I'm Tara."

"I'm Amelia and this is my half-brother, George. He lives in Chicago too, with my dad and stepmother. Maybe you know them, Quentin and Clara?"

Tara's face split into a wide smile. "I know George and of course I know your dad and Aunt Clara. I've even met your sister. Cleo, right?"

I didn't know what to say. Everyone knew everyone else — except for me.

"I have a half-brother too," Tara added. "Only he's older, not cute and little. His name is Justin."

Finally! Someone I'd met, if only for a second.

"Oh, I know him! I mean, I just met him today. Is he nice? What's it like having an older half-brother?"

Tara didn't look like Justin and she didn't have a jelly-roll nose either. →
she seemed nice — at least she was someone to talk to. ←

Tara wrinkled her nose. "I guess it's okay. We fight a lot. Dad says that's what brothers and sisters do, but I don't fight as much with my younger sister. I think it's because we have different moms, and Justin only lives with us half of the time, every other week. Plus, he hates my mom, so it's more peaceful when he's gone." She sighed. "At least my mom doesn't have kids from _her_ first marriage. My best friend has 3 half-siblings – one from her mom and two from her dad. It's a mess!"

And I thought _my_ family was complicated! I guess everyone feels that way.

"So my mom is your dad's sister. We see your family a lot since we all live in Chicago. But everyone else here..." Tara shrugged. "Some of them I see only once a year. And some I've never met before. Like you." She stared at me so intently I felt like something was wrong with my face.

Why are you looking at me like that?
Is something the matter?
I was pretty sure I looked okay.
No embarrassing stains or smudges. Maybe she didn't like my hat.

"You're not what I expected, not how Cleo described you," she said.

I rolled my eyes. "I bet. That's probably a good thing."

Before we could say anything else, Dad came up.

"There you are! I've been looking everywhere for you." He gave Tara a quick kiss, then told us it was time to eat. I wasn't sure whether I liked Tara or not, but I was definitely hungry and I wanted to eat with _someone_ I knew, not just a bunch of strangers.

Everyone was streaming toward lines of tables that had been set up under awnings. I saw Cleo already sitting next to Justin and stuffing corn bread in her mouth. I noticed she hadn't saved a seat for me.

All I saw were unfamiliar faces until Grandpa waved and caught my eye. Grandma called us over, saying she'd saved us places. Clara looked relieved to see us and jumped up to take George. I realized I hadn't seen her talk to anyone. Maybe she felt as uncomfortable at this reunion as I did.

Dad sat next to Clara and introduced me to his sister, Marta, her husband, Michael, and their daughter, Tina - Tara's sister. Tina stuck her tongue out at me.

Tara nudged me and hissed in my ear. "Okay, I fight with her, too, but you can see why, can't you?"

I nodded, waiting for the lump in my throat to go down, but it was lodged tight. I didn't think I could swallow anything. I felt so alone while Cleo looked completely comfortable, laughing with Justin and shoveling down food.

"Amelia, you're sitting next to me," Grandpa insisted. "We have a *lot* of catching up to do."

He winked at me and I felt better right away, just with that little wink. →

I know your dad hasn't told you any of the family stories - like how my parents came to America, what life was like before then...

Marta groaned. "Dad, don't bore her first thing. You'll scare her off this family and she'll never want to visit us again."

"No," I said, my voice suddenly unstuck, the lump gone. "I want to hear the stories. Please tell me." I waited. "Please, Grandpa?" There, I'd said it - Grandpa.

He beamed like he'd been waiting to hear those words.

"That's my girl." He turned to Cleo on the other side of the table "How about you, Cleo? You haven't heard the family history either."

"Thanks, Grandpa," Cleo said, the word sliding like butter out of her mouth. Easy for her! Everything was easier for her! "But Justin and I are going on a hayride as soon as we finish lunch. Later, okay?"

I could tell Grandpa was disappointed, but he just nodded. "Go have fun," he said.

Cleo wiped her barbeque-saucy hands and leaped up. Justin followed her. It was enough to make me want to puke, but Marta thought they were "adorable." She said Justin had been looking forward to the reunion for weeks because of Cleo. I wished somebody had felt that way about me. Suddenly Cleo's fantasy of being the star of the show didn't seem so silly — she was certainly the star of Justin's show.

Cleo got an adoring fan and I got family stories. It didn't seem fair.

Cleo, blowing kisses at her doting public.
SMACK!
SMACK!
Thank you, thank you, everyone! I love you all!
Cleo

Grandpa made a toast, thanking everyone for coming. He named the people who had traveled the farthest and who the new babies were. He didn't mention me and Cleo. I couldn't figure it out - was I part of this family or not?

Then Dad introduced me to his other brother, Jerome, and to his other sister, Julia. At least they got my name right and they didn't say anything mean about Mom. Harold came over too, trying to be all jokey and friendly. I wasn't sure about my other aunts and uncles, but I definitely didn't like him.

No hard feelings, eh, Amelia? I've always liked your mother— she's really something else. You have to understand, divorce is hard on everyone. It's never easy when there are kids involved.

If he said one more cliché, I swear I was going to scream. Lucky for him, he didn't. Instead he invited us over to his house the next day for a big post-reunion brunch. I groaned. That was the last thing I wanted— more reunion after this reunion. I just wanted to go home. I was so relieved when Dad said we had other plans.

"What plans?" I asked after Harold finally walked away.

"NOT going to his house for brunch," Dad said. "ANYTHING but that!" He winked at me.

I laughed. And just that little thing made me love Dad more than ever. I felt like he was on my side and always would be.

The rest of the afternoon there were games like sack races, 3-legged races, bingo, charades, that kind of thing. It was actually fun because I didn't have to talk to anyone. And sometimes it was like being in a big soap opera. After spending several hours with Dad's family I realized there were all kinds of hidden stories and crazy relationships.

FAMILY SECRETS
The wives of Dad's brothers hated each other.
She thinks she's so great!
What a snob!
Clara thought everyone hated her, but they didn't - they just weren't friendly.
Why don't they like me?
What have I done?

Harold's kids terrorized Marta's kids — especially Tyler. He was a total bully.

Did Grandpa give you any money? Cough it up! NOW!
Leave us alone!

Tara told me some of these secrets but some I figured out on my own.

Marta, great seeing you again! Putting on some weight there, eh?
And Michael— whoa! Will you look at that gray hair! Must be from dealing with those kids— a real handful, I'm sure.

It's not true that Harold had a good side, like Grandpa said. Either side is yucchy. No one likes him because he's hypercompetitive, always showing off his latest toy (today it was a teeny, tiny digital camera), and he's plain old rude. Why does he say these things except to hurt people's feelings? Why does practically everything he says start with "I" or "my"?

Julie's husband, Jeff, is so quiet and shy, no one talks to him. I think he should get together with Clara. Then they'd both feel better.

Um, hello... excuse me... um, good-bye...

It all made me realize I wasn't the only one who wasn't sure they belonged. There was no one right way to fit in — it seemed like everyone was finding their own place, even if that place was on the edge of things. Still, there had to be ways to make it easier.

HOW TO SURVIVE FAMILY GET-TOGETHERS IN 10 EASY STEPS!

① Arrive late — traffic is always a good excuse, no matter what time of day it is, rush hour or not.

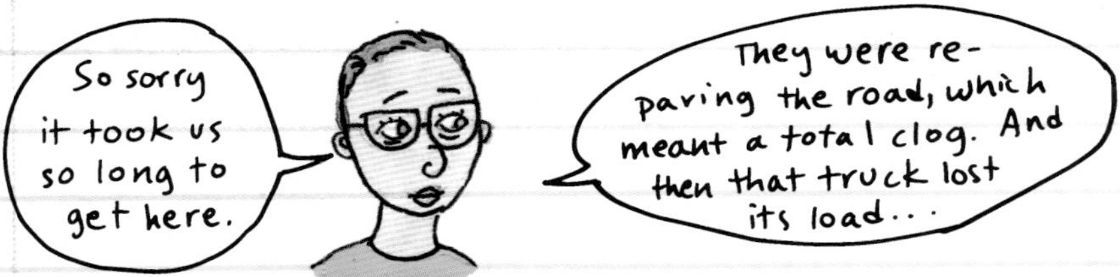

So sorry it took us so long to get here.
They were repaving the road, which meant a total clog. And then that truck lost its load...

② Wear makeup that discourages people from getting too close.

This? On my cheeks? Yes, I'm seeing a doctor about it. No one can quite figure out what it is yet.
Don't worry — doubt

③ Talk in a thick accent so it's hard for anyone to understand what you're saying.

*translation: "I love to read, don't you?"

④ Ask a lot of questions. People love to talk about themselves and that way you don't have to tell them anything about <u>your</u>self.

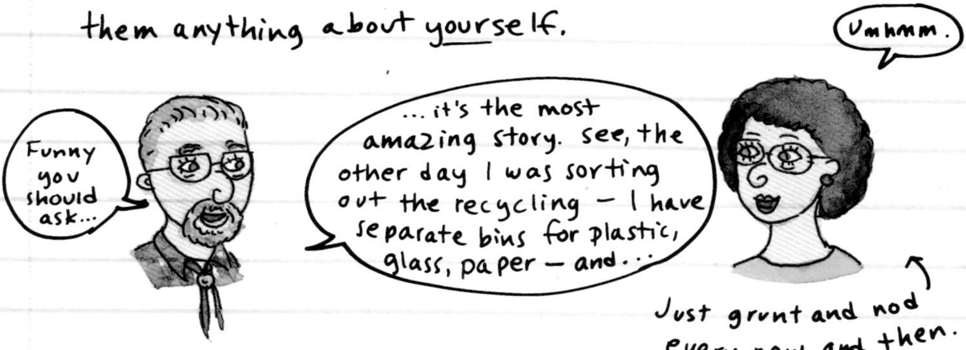

⑤ Eat – no one expects you to talk with your mouth full.

⑥ Spend time at the drinks table. Mix up experiments, potions, whatever.

⑦ Spend time under the drinks table.

⑧ If you're really bored, go out to the parking lot and try to match the people to their cars.

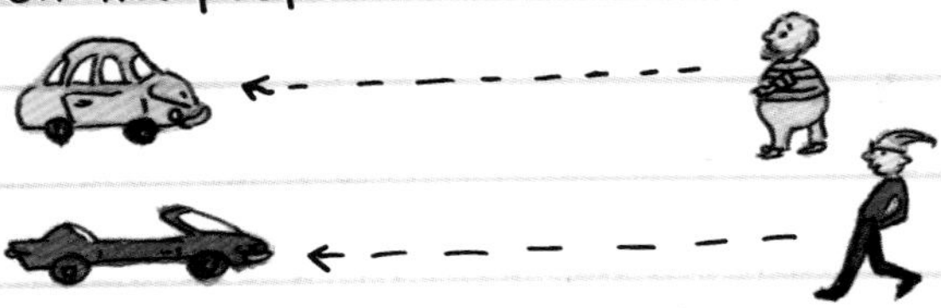

⑨ Make future plans that you have no intention of keeping.

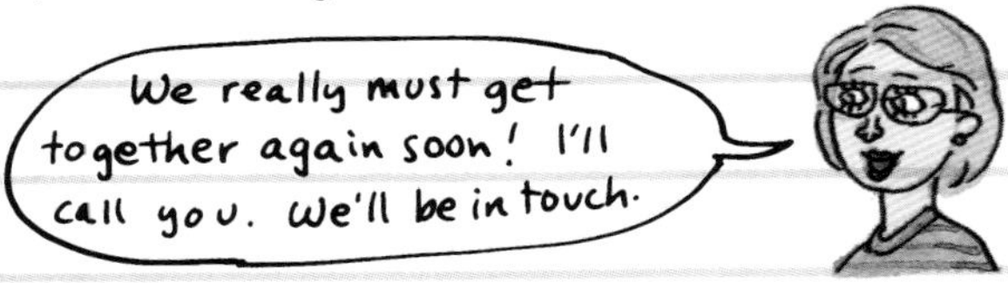

⑩ Leave early.

Or you can use the Cleo method – escape by spending the whole time with one other person. That method has its own risks, however, if you're not sure how you and the other person will get along for that much time. For Cleo and Justin, that wasn't an issue.

I thought a cat had had a litter of kittens in the hay, something like that, but nooooooo, it wasn't that. It was Cleo and Justin, sitting in the barn,

K – I – S – S – I – N – G!

Dad turned purple, Clara was bright pink, Marta was red, and her husband, Michael, was a sickly yellow. Cleo and Justin were surprised. Tara was triumphant.

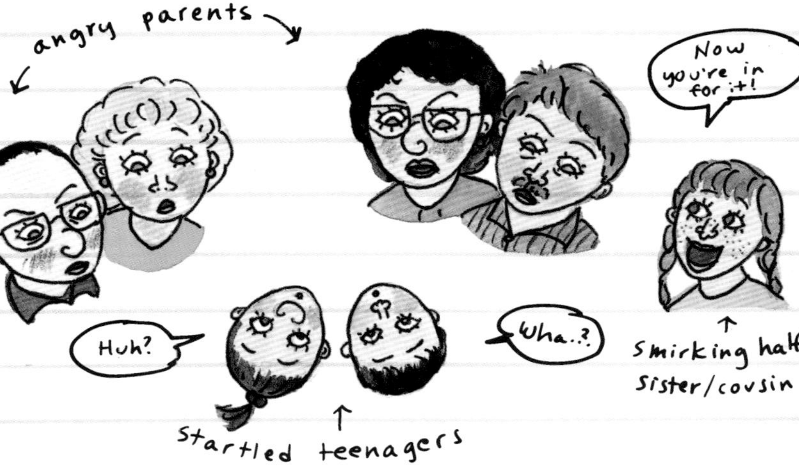

The rest of the reunion, all we heard were "kissing cousin" jokes (even though Justin isn't a <u>real</u> cousin). We didn't stay long after that. Dad rushed us all back to the hotel. He was so mad, he didn't know what to say. I felt sorry for him. He's a great dad with George, but he's not used to older kids. Teenagers are beyond him. Especially one like Cleo.

I have to admit, I kind of admired her. She knew how to get what she wanted.

What's the big crime?
She sulked the whole drive back.

That night Dad gave us both a big lecture about cousins and boyfriends and kissing. It was awful — I didn't want to hear any of it and neither did Cleo. We just nodded and said "Yes, uh huh, we understand" until he left. YUCCH!

Once he was gone, I teased Cleo. "I don't think that's what Dad meant by a family reunion."

Cleo stuck out her tongue at me. "Ha, ha, very funny. The worst part is, he'll tell Mom."

I hadn't thought of that. "So?" I shrugged. "What can she do?"

"Never let me out of her sight again!" Cleo huffed. "They both have to leave me alone and let me grow up!"

I got the feeling that what Cleo wanted was a family un-union — at least from Mom and Dad.

I slept on the floor that night on a pile of blankets. It was better than the bed or the bathroom floor.

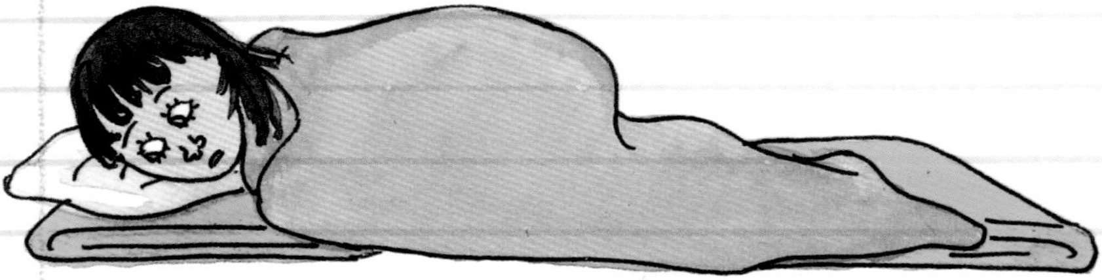

But I couldn't fall asleep. My head was too full of everything that had happened. Now that it was all over, I wondered if it was good I'd come or not.

Should I have stayed home? I was glad I'd met my grandparents. It was good to get a sense of family history from Grandpa's stories. And now Dad's relatives weren't a mystery to me. I still wasn't sure whether I liked some of them or not, but they definitely weren't scary.

All these images flashed through my head.

Chloe?
Adelia?
Uncle Harold, being rude
Grandpa, winking at me
Goat!
George, all excited about the animals
You're not what I expected.
Tara, staring at me

Hey, Cleo!
Justin, ignoring me
Thank you, thank you!
Cleo
Clara, sitting by herself, looking lonely
Cleo, blowing kisses as the star of the show
The baby horse, scrambling to stand up
The games and races
Cleo and Justin, kissing
Dad, looking old and sad and completely confused

Somehow when you talk to someone while you're in bed, in the dark, everything sounds more secret and important and dramatic. It's a great feeling.

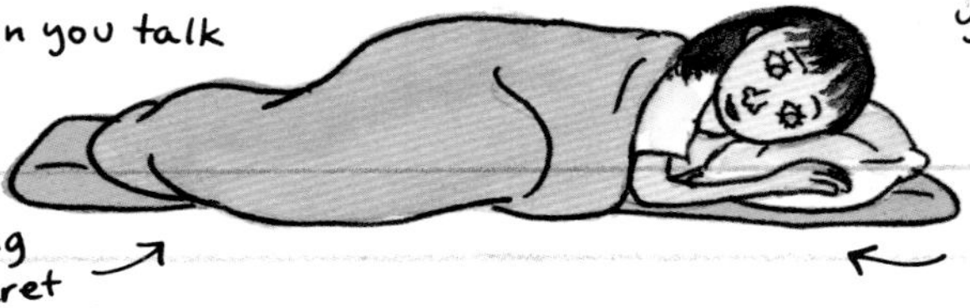

You can barely see the other person so their voice takes on a huge presence. It's magical!

"Cleo!" I whispered. "Are you awake?"

"If I wasn't before, I would be now. What do you want?"

"Are you glad you came?" I asked.

"Of course! I got to see Justin, didn't I? I just hope I can go to Chicago again and Mom doesn't ground me for life."

"I guess I'm glad I came too," I said, suddenly feeling sure of it. "And I'm glad I came with you this time."

"You are?" Cleo sounded surprised.

"Yeah." I smiled in the dark. "I like the way you see things sometimes. You're the perpetual optimist while I'm the constant worrier."

We talked for a long time - about families and boys and kissing. And a lot about Dad. Now that I've met ALL his family, he felt more part of mine than ever. I might still be figuring out how I fit in with everyone else, but I KNEW I belonged with him, even if we didn't live together, even if he'd missed practically my whole childhood.

It was the perfect end to the longest, biggest, most-fights-ever family reunion.

I was feeling so good about Cleo, I didn't even mind the flight home with her, but by the next day we were back to normal, fighting with each other like we always do. Mom was happy to have us back home – she was so happy, she didn't seem mad about Justin even. She thought the whole thing was hilarious.

That'll give your father a taste of raising teenagers – teenage girls!
I wonder if he'll be so eager to have you visit now!

↑ Like she was sure nothing like that would ever happen while she's in charge. She might be in for as much of a surprise as Dad was.

And I got a postcard from Nadia! ↓

Dear Amelia,

How did the family reunion go? I hope it was a lot of fun. I know how tricky those things can be. At the last one our family had, my aunt walked out in a huff after my uncle insulted her taste in books, and one of my cousins bit another cousin. It was more like going to the zoo than going to a party! luv, Nadia – yours till the sun beams!

Amelia
564 N. Homerest
Oopa, Oregon
97881

I smiled — that's how families are. But even the worst people have something good about them — like Cleo (though I still couldn't figure out what it was in Uncle Harold's case).

Carly couldn't wait to hear what happened.

She invited me to spend the night so we could talk all we wanted. I couldn't wait to tell her!

I brought her back a souvenir from Texas — the cowboy hat. She loved it!

We talked until I could see the moon rising outside her bedroom window. I told her about that last night in the hotel with Cleo, how great it was.

"Like it is with us now?" Carly asked. "When we tell each other everything?"

"Yeah," I said. "Just like now."

Neither of us said anything for a while. I was feeling how lucky I was with all my families — Cleo and Mom, Dad, Clara, and George, and here with Carly, my family of friends.

Finally Carly broke the silence. "Good night, Amelia."

"Good night," I whispered back.

And it was.

To Bridget,
who knows how complicated and wonderful families can be.

SIMON & SCHUSTER BOOKS FOR YOUNG READERS
An imprint of Simon & Schuster Children's Publishing Division
1230 Avenue of the Americas, New York, New York 10020

A Paula Wiseman Book

Book design by Amelia
(with help from Lucy Ruth Cummins)
The text for this book is hand-lettered.
Manufactured in the United States of America
2 4 6 8 10 9 7 5 3 1
CIP data for this book is available from the Library of Congress.

ISBN-13: 978-0-689-87447-5 ISBN-10: 0-689-87447-2

first edition